THIS BOOK
BELONGS TO

My Dear Reader,

THIS IS A STORY about a girl named
Beatrix Potter and what happened when
she borrowed her neighbor's guinea pig.

So if you are about to lend your
favorite hamster, snake, cat, turtle,
or hedgehog, please wait! You might
change your mind. . . .

For the Congers—Deniz, Austin, Ayse, and Ayla . . .
and, of course, Bijou, because everyone knows pets are
part of the family —D.H.

For my mother, who was happy with just a cat —C.V.

BEATRIX POTTER

& THE UNFORTUNATE TALE
OF A BORROWED GUINEA PIG

BY DEBORAH HOPKINSON

ILLUSTRATED BY CHARLOTTE VOAKE

schwartz & wade books · new york

MISS BEATRIX POTTER lived with her parents and her little brother, Bertram, at 2 Bolton Gardens in London. Beatrix and Bertram had the whole third floor of the house for their own playroom, science laboratory, and art studio—all in one. It was also a menagerie. For you see, Beatrix probably had more pets than any young lady in the city. But the sad truth is that although Beatrix loved animals, she did not always have the best of luck with them.

Rabbits were Beatrix's favorite animals. She loved to train them, draw them, and paint them. She named her first bunny Benjamin Bouncer.

Later came Peter Piper.

Her bunnies went everywhere with her and were quite happy to stroll along the streets of London on a leash.

Here are a few of Beatrix's other pets (some of whom I am quite sure she and her brother smuggled up the back stairs):

a canary,

a duck,

and a frog called Punch;

salamanders and lizards,
including one named Judy;

hedgehogs, newts,

and a snake named Sally;

a tortoise,

a wild duck,

a jay, and a kestrel.

Now, as I imagine you know, most wild creatures don't like being cooped up in a house. So Beatrix was continually recording the latest disaster in her journal.

A day of misfortunes . . . Sally and four black newts escaped overnight. Caught one black newt in school room and another in larder, but nothing seen of poor Sally. . . .

Beatrix could only hope Sally had not fallen into the clutches of another member of the menagerie.

That is precisely what happened to a bat that Bertram had captured and put in a small wooden box. Beatrix confided to her diary:

The very next morning that horrid old jack jay, being left alone to bathe in a wash basin, opened the box and destroyed the poor creature. I fancy he found it ill-favored, but he pulled out its arms and legs in a disgusting fashion.

The worst was yet to come.

One dark day Beatrix witnessed the passing
of an entire family of snails, and all their
friends besides. She wrote:

*An awful tragedy was discovered . . .
the whole Bill family, old Bill and Mrs. Little
Bill, and ditto Grimes and Sextis Grimes his
wife, Lord and Lady Salisbury, Mr. and Mrs.
Camfield, Mars and Venus, and three or four*

*others were every one dead and
dried up. . . . I am very much put
out about the poor things.*

Beatrix had only herself to blame.

*They were all asleep in bed and
it seemed so cruel to water them.*

Now we come to the heart of our story—the tale of the unfortunate guinea pig. Why Beatrix needed to borrow one is quite simple: while she enjoyed playing with her pets, her greatest joy came from painting them.

Beatrix spent long hours sketching her animals. She liked to paint them doing ordinary, everyday things, like reading the newspaper, working in the garden, or taking tea. (And why not?)

Then came the day when Beatrix decided she absolutely, positively needed to make some pictures of a guinea pig. Donning a smart hat, she knocked on the door of her neighbor Miss Nina Paget.

"Please, Miss Paget, you would do me a great favor if you could lend me one of your guinea pigs to paint," Beatrix begged. "I promise it will come to no harm."

Miss Paget led Beatrix into the parlor. "Which little darling did you have in mind?" she asked.

"I would love to draw Queen Elizabeth," declared Beatrix. "She is truly magnificent."

Her friend beamed. "Her family is indeed impeccable. Queen Elizabeth comes from a long line of distinguished guinea pigs. She is the daughter of Titwillow the Second, and a descendant of the Sultan of Zanzibar and the Light of Asia."

You might well think the young ladies were discussing royalty, not rodents. In the end, Miss Paget was so flattered by Miss Potter's appreciation of the merits of Queen Elizabeth that she eagerly fetched the squealing creature.

"Thank you," said Beatrix. "I will return her—unharmed—in the morning."

Alas, it was an empty promise.

The sitting began quite auspiciously. Beatrix got out her watercolors, placed Queen Elizabeth on the table, and set to work.

At eight o'clock precisely, Beatrix was summoned to a fancy dinner party with her parents and a few guests. "I will return directly, Your Majesty," Beatrix assured the queen as she hurriedly dressed.

Beatrix fidgeted all through the evening. She could hardly wait to get back to her work.

Meanwhile, upstairs, Queen Elizabeth was eating dinner as well. She gobbled up the blotting paper Beatrix kept on her desk to absorb ink from her dip pen.

She consumed some string that lay on the desk to wrap a package.

Then, not quite satisfied, the wretched queen tucked into a stack of writing paper and paste for dessert.

PASTE

When at last Beatrix bounded into her art studio, ready to take up her brush again, a horrible sight met her eyes. "Your Majesty, what have you done?"

She scooped Queen Elizabeth up and put her into a cage. "We will have to finish in the morning," she scolded, and then she went to bed.

Dear Reader,

You can guess what happened next. That repast of paper, paste, and string took its toll. In the night the queen expired.

When Beatrix awoke, she let forth a yelp of distress. "Miss Paget," she cried, "is going to throttle me!"

Miss Paget was indeed displeased when Beatrix appeared
with a box holding a stiff and bloated Queen Elizabeth.

"I am so sorry," wailed Beatrix. She held up the delightful
little watercolor she had made of the late queen.
"Please accept this piece of art as a small token
of apology."

Miss Nina Paget harrumphed, grabbed
the paper, and slammed the door.

Now, Dear Reader;

I'd like you to imagine that you were in Miss Paget's shoes at that moment. Would you have torn the painting to shreds in anger? Or would you have kept it as a reminder of your dearly departed guinea pig?

If you chose to keep it, I think you would be very wise. Here's why:

Beatrix Potter went on to create *The Tale of Peter Rabbit* and other beloved books for children about squirrels, ducks, mice, cats, tortoises, frogs—and, yes, guinea pigs.

She became so famous, in fact, that many years later, a small picture that she made of a guinea pig sold for thousands of pounds. The painting was probably done the same year that she borrowed Queen Elizabeth.

A final reminder:

If you choose to lend a pet (or just about anything) to an aspiring artist of your acquaintance and something unfortunate happens, be sure to get a picture.

And then keep it. Because you just never know.

*I remain
yrs sincerely,
Deborah Hopkinson*

P.S. (Author's Note)

1.

Beatrix Potter (July 28, 1866–December 22, 1943) is famous around the world as the creator of the most beloved animal tales for children ever written. Beatrix began drawing when she was a girl and became skilled at depicting birds, insects, and plants. She also enjoyed working with watercolors.

2.

Beatrix and her little brother, Bertram, both adored animals. Beatrix kept dogs her whole life and had many other pets too. She loved to draw rabbits, mice, and, yes, guinea pigs, from live models.

This story was inspired by entries in the journal Beatrix kept from 1881 to 1897. In it, she often describes mishaps that befell the pets (and various wild creatures) she and Bertram brought home. Beatrix wrote her journal in a secret code, which gave her the privacy to express her thoughts. Many years later, Leslie Linder, an engineer who collected her drawings, was able to decode and transcribe her words. Her journal was published in 1966.

3.

5.

4.

To tell this story, I've added some made-up bits and changed Beatrix's age. (She was actually twenty-six when she borrowed Queen Elizabeth from her neighbor.) I wrote it as a picture letter because that is how Beatrix's own early stories were written. In fact, her first book, *The Tale of Peter Rabbit*, published in 1902, grew out of a picture letter about four little rabbits she sent to a five-year-old boy named Noel Moore in 1893.

While I do not know if Elizabeth Ann Paget (known as Nina) kept the offering of Beatrix's drawing, one of the artist's watercolor drawings of guinea pigs created around this time sold at auction in 2011 for more than $85,000.

In addition to her wonderful children's books, Beatrix left another legacy. With money she made from writing and illustrating, she bought Hill Top Farm in England's Lake District. Eventually she married, and made this beautiful area her home.

Beatrix continued to purchase land to help preserve traditional farms in the Lake District. On her death she donated four thousand acres to Great Britain's National Trust.

Today, Hill Top Farm is a museum. I am sure rabbits roam there still.

Oh, and in case you're wondering, Beatrix wrote many letters in her life, often signing them "I remain yrs sincerely."

MORE ABOUT BEATRIX POTTER

To learn more about Beatrix Potter, visit the Beatrix Potter Society: beatrixpottersociety.org.uk

To read about Beatrix's guinea pig drawing that sold at auction, visit Bonhams: bonhams.com/auctions/18686/lot/2098/

To learn more about the artist and her work at the Victoria and Albert Museum, which holds a large collection of manuscripts and paintings, many of which came to the museum as a bequest from Leslie Linder, and to see a photo of Mr. Linder at work decoding her journal, visit the museum's website: vam.ac.uk/content/articles/t/beatrix-potter-collections/

To find out about the farms and land Beatrix worked to protect, visit the National Trust: nationaltrust.org.uk/beatrix-potter-gallery/things-to-see-and-do/

NOTES AND PERMISSIONS

Quotations from Beatrix Potter's journal are all from *The Journal of Beatrix Potter, 1881–1897,* transcribed from her code writings by Leslie Linder, published by Penguin Group, London, in 1989. Used by permission of Frederick Warne & Co. Page numbers are listed below. Other dialogue has been invented.

"A day of misfortunes" p. 54 (Friday, September 21, 1883)

"The very next morning" p. 362 (Monday, October 8, 1894)

"An awful tragedy" p. 59 (Saturday, December 8, 1883)

Photograph and Art Credits

Frederick Warne & Co. is the owner of all rights, copyrights, and trademarks in the Beatrix Potter character names and illustrations.

1. Beatrix feeding a wire-haired (border) terrier from a plate (1897)
   Princeton University Library
2. Beatrix and her brother, Bertram
   The Beatrix Potter Society
3. Beatrix, aged 15, with Spot (1881)
   © Frederick Warne & Co. 1881
   Courtesy of the Victoria and Albert Museum
4. Beatrix's code writing
   © Frederick Warne & Co. 1966
5. Beatrix with Benjamin Bouncer on a leash (1891)
   Princeton University Library
6. Peter Rabbit Picture Letter
   © Frederick Warne & Co. 1946
   Courtesy of the Frederick Warne Archive
7. Guinea pig watercolor
   Courtesy of Bonhams & Butterfields Auctioneers Corp.
8. Hill Top, Sawrey
   © Frederick Warne & Co. 1966
   Courtesy of the Linder Collection
9. Beatrix at Hill Top Farm (c. 1908)
   © National Trust/Robert Thrift

Text copyright © 2016 by Deborah Hopkinson
Jacket art and interior illustrations copyright © 2016 by Charlotte Voake
All rights reserved. Published in the United States by Schwartz & Wade Books, an imprint of Random House Children's Books, a division of Penguin Random House LLC, New York.
Schwartz & Wade Books and the colophon are trademarks of Penguin Random House LLC.
Visit us on the Web! randomhousekids.com
Educators and librarians, for a variety of teaching tools, visit us at RHTeachersLibrarians.com
Library of Congress Cataloging-in-Publication Data
Hopkinson, Deborah.
Beatrix Potter and the unfortunate tale of a borrowed guinea pig / by Deborah Hopkinson ; illustrated by Charlotte Voake. — First edition.
pages cm
ISBN 978-0-385-37325-8 (hc) — ISBN 978-0-385-37326-5 (glb) — ISBN 978-0-385-37327-2 (ebook)
1. Potter, Beatrix, 1866–1943—Juvenile literature. 2. Authors, English—20th century—Biography—Juvenile literature. I. Voake, Charlotte, illustrator. II. Title.
PR6031.O72Z5874 2015
823'.912—dc23
[B]
2014010931
The text of this book is set in Garamond Premier Bold.
The illustrations were rendered in pen and watercolor.
MANUFACTURED IN CHINA
2 4 6 8 10 9 7 5 3 1
First Edition
Random House Children's Books supports the First Amendment and celebrates the right to read.